Maple and Birch Publishing, LLC
BookiColor® is a registered trademark of Maple and Birch Publishing, LLC.
Patent Pending.

Library of Congress Cataloging-in-Publication Data
Names: Harmon Rourke, Jaime, author. | Rourke, Harmony Jai, author. | Green Harmon, Dr. Rhonda Y., editor.
Title: Harmony and Her Best Friend Rex
Identifiers: Library of Congress Control Number: 2021914318 | ISBN: 978-1-7375318-0-7 (hardcover) | ISBN: 978-1-7375318-1-4 (eBook)

Our books may be purchased in bulk for promotional, educational, or business use. Please contact Maple and Birch Publishing, LLC Sales Department by email @ mapleandbirchpublishing@gmail.com

For **H**, thank you for being my inspiration and much needed co-pilot in this journey. Always dream big little one. I Love You!

Harmony and Her Best Friend REX

Jaime Harmon Rourke and
Harmony Jai Rourke

Harmony loved to play with her best friend, Rex, the T-Rex.

Every morning Harmony would wake up, grab Rex, potty, brush, and then they would eat their favorite breakfast.

After eating breakfast, Rex would magically come to life, but the only one who knew Rex was alive was Harmony.

Harmony would read her favorite
dinosaur books with Rex.

Sing her favorite songs with Rex and eat her favorite ice cream with Rex.

Stomp and Roar with Rex!

Ride her bike with Rex.

Eat lunch with Rex.

But one day, when Harmony woke up from her nap, Rex was gone.

Harmony looked under the bed, in the closet, and in their favorite hiding place, the pink castle tent. But still no Rex.

Rex was swimming and doing flips in their pool! Harmony couldn't believe her eyes. No one else knew Rex was alive, at least she thought. But she heard her mommy laugh.

Harmony ran out of her room and into the kitchen, where she saw her mommy standing in the window and laughing at Rex swimming and doing flips in their pool. Harmony said, "Mommy, how can you see, Rex?"

Mommy told Harmony when I was your age Rex was my best friend, and now he is your best friend. One day when you are a mommy, he will be your little's best friend too.

Fascinating Facts about the Tyrannosaurus Rex!!
(Tye-RAN-uh-SAWR-us)

The Tyrannosaurus Rex, or as we fondly call the dinosaur, the T-Rex, roamed the planet during the Late Cretaceous Period over 65 million years ago. The name Tyrannosaurus Rex comes from the Greek and Latin words meaning 'Tyrant Lizard King.'

The T-Rex is known as one of the greatest predators who ever lived. The T-Rex had powerful back legs that allowed it to hunt its prey over short distances at up to 20 mph.

T-Rex was an enormous (length up to 40 feet and weighed 6.7 tons) carnivore (meat-eating dinos), but they were not the biggest!

Some of the more giant dinosaurs were the Giganotosaurus (length up to 43 feet), Carcharodontosaurus (length up to 46 feet), and the Spinosaurus (length up to 52 feet). Wow! Amazing!

The largest T-Rex tooth found was approximately 12 inches long.

The T-Rex had binocular vision, which allowed them to locate prey with great precision.

T-Rex's arms were short and powerful.

The T-Rex walked on slim, birdlike feet.

Fascinating facts are still being discovered about the T-Rex every day.

T-Rex Fascinating Facts Quiz

1. What period did the T-Rex roam the planet?
2. What length was the T-Rex?
3. How many inches was the T-Rex's tooth that was found?
4. How much does a T-Rex weigh?
5. What were three dinosaurs more enormous than the T-Rex?
6. What are the Greek and Latin words meaning T-Rex?

LET'S ADD SOME COLOR

About the Authors

As a mother of a lover of dinosaurs and all things Science, Jaime Harmon Rourke decided to write her first children's book with the assistance of and inspired by her daughter Harmony. Her love for writing began as a child. Her journey started when she wrote her first book in the third grade and has loved reading and writing ever since. Jaime has a B.S. in Criminal Justice, M.S. in Criminal Justice and M.B.A. in International Business. Jaime lives on the Atlantic coast with her husband, her daughter Harmony and her mom and dad.

Harmony Jai Rourke is a very active, curious little girl who enjoys reading and pretending to be a Paleontologist. She also loves to pretend to be a mighty T-Rex, her favorite dinosaur. When Harmony grows up, she has plans to become a doctor.

Sources

Castro, Joseph. (2016). Giganotosaurus: Facts About the 'Giant Southern Lizard.'
https://www.livescience.com

Facts Just For Kids. Tyrannosaurus Rex Facts. https://www.factsjustforkids.com

Hibbert, C. (2019). Children's Encyclopedia of Dinosaurs.

Kids-dinosaurs.com Where did Tyrannosaurus Rex Live? https://www.kids-dinosaurs.com

Stevens, Kent A. (2006). Binocular vision in theropod dinosaurs. Journal of Vertebrate Paleontology.26(2).https://www.researchgate.net/publication/228671730_Binocular_vision_in_theropod_dinosaurs
DOI:10.1671/0272-4634(2006)26[321:BVITD]2.0.CO:2

The Teeth of 25 Dinosaurs and Other Prehistoric Creatures. https://www.mainstreetsmiles.com

Wikipedia https://en.m.wikipedia.org